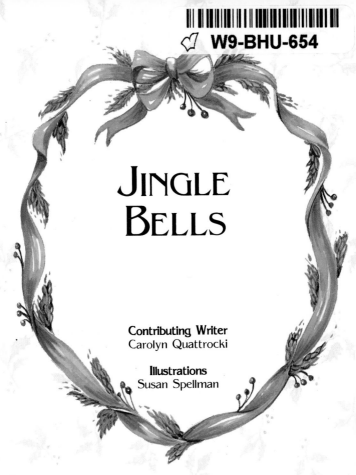

JINGLE BELLS

Contributing Writer
Carolyn Quattrocki

Illustrations
Susan Spellman

Publications International, Ltd.

Toby was mad. "It isn't fair!" he said as he stomped around the kitchen.

Jeb and Harriet, his older brother and sister, always had all the fun. And tonight they were going out *again* on a sleigh ride with the older boys and girls from some of the farms nearby. Toby couldn't go along because he was "too little." Would he *ever* not be "too little" for all the things he wanted to do?

Mama shook her head and smiled. "Time for bed," she said. "Maybe next year you'll be big enough to go."

Toby went up to the bedroom he shared with baby Sarah. "Look how much bigger I am than Sarah. Why do Harriet and Jeb always do things together and I get stuck with a *baby!*" But Mama just hugged Toby. Then she tucked Toby and Sarah under their quilts and kissed them goodnight.

Just as Toby closed his eyes, he heard a jingling noise outside. He jumped out of bed and looked out his window. He was just in time to see Harriet and Jeb climbing into a sleigh pulled by a beautiful, brown horse.

The sleigh was full of laughing boys and girls. As it pulled away from the door of his house, Toby could hear the riders begin to sing, "*Dashing through the snow, in a one-horse open sleigh. . .*"

The next day was Christmas Eve. Papa called to Harriet and Jeb, "This morning we must go to the woods and cut down our Christmas tree." Toby wished he could go, too, but Papa said he was "too little."

Toby was so disappointed. Then Mama had an idea! While the others went for the tree, she and Toby made long strings of red cranberries to use as decorations. It wasn't such a bad morning after all.

Just before lunch, Papa and Harriet and Jeb came stomping into the house, half covered with snow. They were dragging a huge tree.

That afternoon, Papa set up the tree in the parlor. The whole family put colored balls and sparkling tinsel on it. Then Toby proudly presented his long strings of cranberries to put on the tree. He was sure that his decorations were the prettiest ones of all.

That night, Harriet, Jeb, and Toby hung their stockings on the fireplace. They also hung a little red and white striped stocking for baby Sarah, because she was too small to do it herself.

Then Mama said, "Now it's off to bed for Toby and Sarah." Toby thought about begging to stay up later. But he decided not to. Because, after all, tomorrow would be Christmas!

But after Toby was in bed, he had barely closed his eyes when Papa and Mama came into the room. "Don't go to sleep quite yet, little ones," Papa said to Toby and Sarah. "Mama and Harriet and Jeb and I have a big surprise for you."

Mama and Papa carried Toby and Sarah, wrapped in blankets, to the door of their house. There, sitting right in front, was a beautiful sleigh decorated with silvery bells!

The whole family piled into the sleigh. Soon they were speeding along in the open fields to the clip-clop of the horse's hooves and the jingling of bells. As they rode along, they sang:

Dashing through the snow,
  in a one-horse open sleigh,

O'er the fields we go,
  laughing all the way.

Bells on bob-tail ring,
  making spirits bright,

What fun it is to ride and sing
  a sleighing song tonight!

*Jingle Bells, jingle bells,
 jingle all the way.*
*Oh, what fun it is to ride
 in a one-horse open sleigh!*

As they started back toward
home, Papa eased the horse
down to a slow trot. Toby
leaned his head against Papa's
big shoulder. He smiled up at
Papa and whispered, "This is the
best Christmas surprise I've
ever had!"

And as Toby's eyes drifted
slowly shut, he softly sang to
himself, *"jingle all the way..."*